For PZapp, and G & Scotty
With endless gratitude to Deborah Warren and Sarah Rockett
—Erin

For Sarah
—Claire

Text Copyright © 2019 Erin Dealey
Illustration Copyright © 2019 Claire Shorrock
Design Copyright © 2019 Sleeping Bear Press

Sleeping Bear Press™
2395 South Huron Parkway, Suite 200, Ann Arbor, MI 48104
www.sleepingbearpress.com
© Sleeping Bear Press

Printed and bound in China.
10 9 8 7 6 5 4 3 2 1

Library of Congress Cataloging-in-Publication Data
Names: Dealey, Erin, author. | Shorrock, Claire, illustrator.
Title: Snow globe wishes / by Erin Dealey ; illustrated by Claire Shorrock.
Description: Ann Arbor, MI : Sleeping Bear Press, [2019] | Summary: After the worst snowstorm
of the year, a young girl wishes on a snow globe that everyone will come out to play
and share a dream of peace. | Identifiers: LCCN 2019010254 | ISBN 9781534110311 (hardcover)
Subjects: | CYAC: Stories in rhyme. | Snow--Fiction. | Community life--Fiction. | Wishes--Fiction.
Classification: LCC PZ8.3.D3415 Sno 2019 | DDC [E]--dc23
LC record available at https://lccn.loc.gov/2019010254

snow globe wishes

By Erin Dealey · Pictures by Claire Shorrock

Published by Sleeping Bear Press

Lights go out!
Fierce clouds blow in.
Garlands fly on frozen wind.

Lost connections—
phones, computers.

Bundled, homeward-bound commuters.

Traffic slows. Roads disappear
     beneath the worst storm of the year.

Picnic dinners,
candlelight.
Darkness draws us close tonight.

Blanket forts.

Crawl in.
Scoot over.

Kitten purrs.
Me, too! barks Rover.

Snow globe wishes.
Close your eyes.

Snowplows rumble lullabies.

Then slowly stretching,
morning yawns.
Look!
Brilliant skies, rose-golden dawn.

Wake up! A whisper from the snow.
Do you hear its soft *Hello?*

Magic sparkles,
beckons, swirls—

Come outside,
dear boys and girls!

Children hear it best, they say.
But,
what if
on this snow globe day...?

Families shake their busy lives.
Heavy doors fling open wide.

And out they go—
ones, twos,
threes, fours—

in cities, towns,
and right next door.

Outside to winter's wonderland!

Who'll be the first to grab a hand

that grabs a hand
and then another—
neighbors, strangers, sisters, brothers?

What if,
dear friends,
on this snow globe day
EVERYONE comes out to play?

To share a smile,
to catch the spirit—
laugh until the world can hear it.

And pass it on
as bright eyes glisten.
Do you hear what they hear?
Listen . . .

Peace on earth.
Right now.
Right here.

Peace for all
throughout the year!